Mouse Tells the Truth

Written by
Ella Law

Illustrated by
Laura Vitória Jäger

Owl's house

High Hill

Goat's house

Rabbit's burrow

The "Big Hole"

Meadow

Squirrel's
treehouse

Wood

Mouse's
house

Cave

Park

Rainbow Island

2

Lighthouse

Mole's house

Badger's boathouse

Fox's den

Beach

Harbour

N
W   E
S

3

Hello,

On Rainbow Island, we like everyone to be friends. It's a lovely place to live and it's important we all feel safe and happy. And that's why we have the Kindness Club. When you show kindness, it makes you and your friends feel good.

All the animals want to join the Kindness Club but first they have to show real kindness to their friends. Then, as a reward, they can become a member and even get a special Kindness Club badge that reminds them to be kind every day.

It's not always easy to be kind, but everyone on Rainbow Island agrees that when you are, it makes you feel wonderful!

So why don't you try to show kindness every day, too. And if you're lucky, you might even get your very own Kindness Club badge!

Love,
Badger x

Meet the animals on Rainbow Island

Fox

Fox really likes a challenge. She's great fun but can get a bit too excited. Her favourite place on Rainbow Island is the lighthouse.

Badger

Badger has lived on Rainbow Island for a very long time. He has a boathouse on the harbour and organizes trips around the island on his boat.

Goat

Goat is not afraid to say what he thinks. He likes to keep busy and gets up early every morning to do his exercises outdoors.

Squirrel

Squirrel likes to cook vegetables from the fields and nuts and berries from the woods. He also bakes the best chocolate cake on Rainbow Island!

Rabbit

Rabbit just loves playing with her friends, especially at the outdoor play area in the park. She thinks Rainbow Island is the best place in the world!

Mouse

Mouse loves an adventure. He may be small but he's very brave. His two favourite things are boats and picnics!

Mole

Mole likes to have her say and often comes up with great ideas. She loves exploring Rainbow Island at night.

Owl

Owl has just learnt to fly and often fetches Badger if one of her friends is in trouble. She knows all the best beaches on the island!

5

It was a beautiful, sunny morning.

Mouse was **bursting** with excitement as he was going on a boat trip with his friends.

He'd been up extra early to make a picnic with lots of tasty treats for Fox and Goat and delicious nutty snacks for Squirrel and Mole.

As he waited for his friends,
Mouse started to play with the oar.

Suddenly he had a
brilliant idea.

"I'll show them all
I'm not too small
to row!" he shouted.

Mouse pressed the oar against the side of the boat and gave a huge **PUSH.**

"Whoah!"

he laughed, as the boat started to swing.

BANG! Mouse felt his heart jump into his throat.

Then he saw the small hole at the bottom of the boat.

"What am I going to do?" he wailed.

Mouse struggled to move the boat again. He wished he was stronger.

He **pushed** and **pushed** and finally he was able to press the oar against the harbour wall.

The little boat **swung around** and soon it was back in place.

Suddenly he heard voices. His friends were coming!

"I'm rowing today!" called Fox.

"No, I am!" cried Goat.

Mouse quickly placed his picnic basket over the hole. His heart began to pound very **loudly**.

11

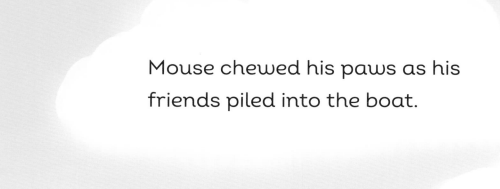

Mouse chewed his paws as his friends piled into the boat.

There were loud **shrieks** and **giggles** as they fell on top of each other.

13

Finally they were ready to go. It didn't take long for Fox to show off her rowing.

"Slow down!" shouted Goat. "You'll hit that rock!"

Fox had to **swerve** quickly.

"My feet are wet!"
cried Squirrel as water
poured into the boat.

Mouse felt sick
with worry as he
watched his picnic
basket float by.

Goat found the hole in the bottom of the boat.

"I told you not to go so fast," he warned Fox.

Moments later, Squirrel squealed. "The hole's getting

bigger!"

16

"**Help!**" cried Rabbit, as the water gushed in.

Mouse said nothing. He had a very strange feeling in his tummy.

Owl flew off to find help.

17

Fox carefully steered the boat to a little bay.
Just as they arrived, Badger appeared.
Clever Owl had kindly gone to fetch him.

"Fox **crashed** our boat!"
Goat called to Badger.

Fox looked
very upset.

"It was an accident," said Squirrel, kindly.
"And Fox got us here safely in the end."

"Our picnic's ruined and I'm
very **wet!**" cried Rabbit.

"You'll dry out quickly in the
sun," Badger reassured them.

19

"Let's put our picnic blanket down!" cried Goat. Everyone joined in and soon happy chatter rang out.

No one seemed to notice that Mouse stayed **very quiet**.

Mouse was feeling bad that Fox was blamed for spoiling the picnic. He didn't want Fox to be upset.

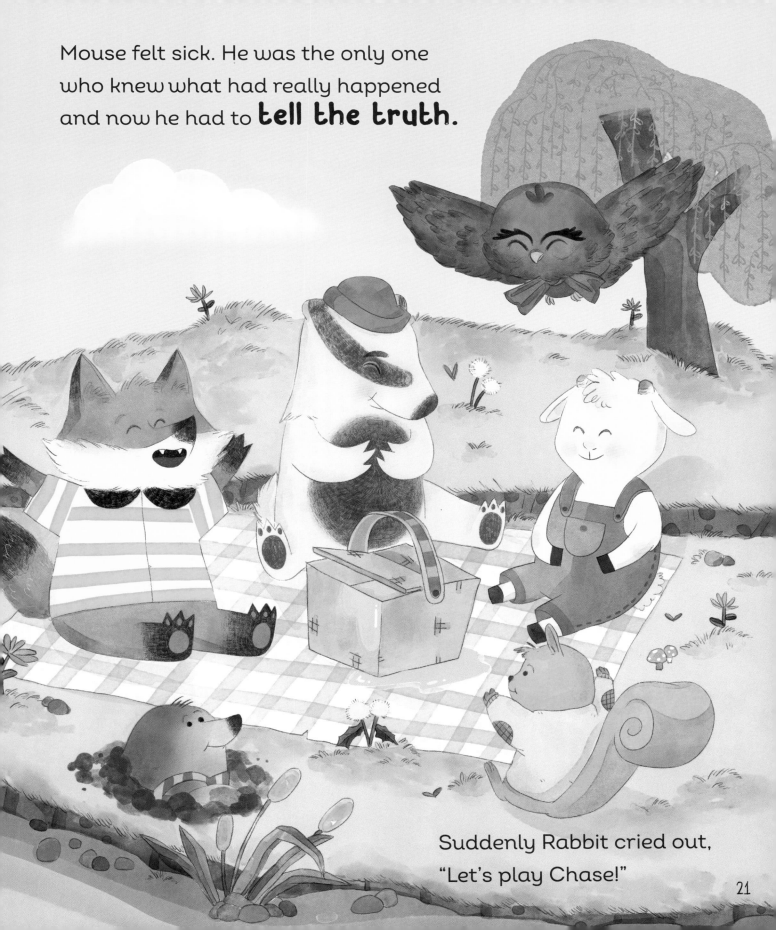

Mouse felt sick. He was the only one who knew what had really happened and now he had to **tell the truth.**

Suddenly Rabbit cried out, "Let's play Chase!"

21

As his friends played in the sun, Mouse stared sadly at the **soggy** sandwiches, the **wet** nuts, and the **damp** fruit.

"What's wrong, Mouse?" Badger asked gently.

Mouse suddenly **burst** into tears.

Everyone crowded round.

"It's not Fox's fault – **it's mine!**"
sobbed Mouse.

Then he told them all how the hole
appeared when he banged the boat.

Everyone was shocked to hear Mouse's story.

"Why didn't you tell us about the
hole in the boat?" asked Rabbit.

"I was afraid you'd all be cross
with me," sobbed Mouse.

"Poor Mouse," said Squirrel,
giving him a **huge hug.**

Badger explained that Mouse hadn't meant to damage the boat. It was just an accident.

"And we need to be **kind** when accidents happen," Badger reminded them all.

"Definitely! I know what will make you feel better, Mouse," said Goat.

"Let's play Hide and Seek!"

25

But first Mouse had something to say to Fox.

"I never wanted you to get the blame, Fox. **I'm sorry** I upset you."

"That's okay, Mouse," said Fox, kindly. "I know you're not mean."

"Well done, Mouse, for saying sorry," said Badger.
"And well done, Fox, for accepting the apology. It's
not nice being blamed for something you didn't do."

"Can we play Hide and
Seek now?" asked Goat.

"Of course!"
laughed Badger.

By the time they finished playing, the sun had dried the picnic.

As the hungry friends tucked in, Badger had something important to say. "Mouse was very brave to tell the truth. He made a mistake and didn't want Fox to be blamed.

Congratulations, Mouse, you're now a member of the

Rainbow Island KINDNESS CLUB. "

As they made their way home on Badger's boat, Mouse was feeling tired but **happy.**

"Now I'm in the Kindness Club, I'm going to be kind **every day,**" he told Badger.

"Being kind can be hard sometimes, Mouse,
so just do your best," said Badger.

And in no time, Mouse was **fast asleep**.

What did you learn?

Mouse found out that telling the truth made him feel so much better. He had lots of different feelings during his adventure, so let's see what you can remember.

- How did Mouse feel when he saw the hole in the boat?

- Why didn't Mouse tell his friends when they arrived about the hole in the boat?

- Why was Goat cross with Fox on the boat?

- How did Mouse feel when the picnic was ruined?

- Why was Mouse very quiet when they were getting the picnic ready?

- Why did Mouse say sorry to Fox?

- Why did Fox forgive Mouse?

- How did Mouse feel when he told everyone he had made the hole in the boat?

- Why did Badger make Mouse a member of the Kindness Club?

- What would you have done if you were Mouse and crashed the boat?

Make your own Kindness Club badge

Trace the badge below and then decorate it however you like.

How can you be kind?

There are lots of different ways you can be kind as the Rainbow Island friends showed us.

Saying sorry

If you've hurt someone's feelings, say sorry and show you were wrong. That's why Mouse said sorry to Fox when she was upset.

Forgiving someone

If someone apologizes for hurting your feelings, it's kind to forgive them. Fox forgave Mouse even though she'd been blamed for something she didn't do.

Doing something to help

When someone needs help, think what you can do. Owl saw the rowing boat would sink and immediately flew off to find Badger so he could take everyone home in his boat.

Understanding accidents can happen

Sometimes accidents happen. When everyone blamed Fox, Squirrel was kind to explain it was an accident. And later, Badger made it clear that Mouse hadn't meant to crash the boat.

Noticing when someone is upset

One of the kindest things you can do is to look out
for how your friends are feeling. If they are upset,
you could try to cheer them up, just like Goat did.
He knew Mouse was upset about the boat,
so suggested they all play Hide and Seek.

Tell the truth

Always tell the truth. That way, no one will be hurt or blamed for
something they didn't do. Mouse knew she had to tell the truth in the
end – and she felt so much better when she did.

Be kind to yourself

It's great to be kind to others, but don't forget to be kind to yourself,
too. So if you do something good, congratulate yourself, just like
Mouse did when she was given the Kindness Club badge.

Make your own Kindness Rainbow

And show you're as kind as the Rainbow Island animals.

You will need:

2 x A4 sheet white paper
1 plate
Pencil
⚠ Safety scissors (Ask a grown-up for help with the scissors)
Glue stick
1 x A4 card, sky blue colour

Here's what to do:

1. Place the plate on a sheet of white paper so only half the plate is on the paper. This should form a semicircle, taking up about half of the page.

2. Draw a line in pencil around the semicircle.

⚠

3. Ask a grown-up to help you cut out a semicircle. This will be your rainbow.

4. Colour in your rainbow starting at the centre with purple followed by blue, green, yellow, orange and, finally, red.

5. Glue the rainbow to the bottom of the blue card. Make sure you only glue up to the orange line – it is important that the red line is not glued as this is where the Kindness notes will be placed.

6. Take the second sheet of white paper and draw two large fluffy clouds in pencil.

7. Ask a grown-up to help you cut out the clouds and glue to the blue card above the rainbow.

8. The cloud on the left is for your name. On the other cloud, write Kindness Rainbow.

9. And now for the exciting part ... every time you do a kind thing, write it down on small piece of paper (or ask a grown-up to help) and place it behind the red line of the rainbow. Then you can see all the kind things you've done!

Notes for grown-ups

As parents or carers, we strive to impart values to our little ones and at the heart of these values is kindness. We all know how very young children learn through mimicking behaviour around them – and they couldn't have better role models than the Rainbow Island characters in the Kindness Club!

Here are some tips on how to get the most out of the series:

Reading the story

- As you are reading the story, make sure you engage your child by showing how much you are enjoying the story and pictures, too.
- Use different voices for each character so they come alive.
- Encourage your child to guess what might happen next before you turn each page.

Using the supplementary material

- Use the What did you learn? section to talk about the feelings of the different characters. This is an ideal way to ensure your child has not only understood the story but is also able to empathize and has learnt important lessons along the way.

- Use the How can you be kind? section to talk about how to practise these suggestions and also to explain to your child the importance of showing kindness to themselves. Wherever possible, make comparisons between the characters and situations in the story with people your child knows. This link will reinforce the message of the importance of showing kindness.

- Use the Kindness Activities to demonstrate how being kind makes you feel better – and don't forget to congratulate your child for every kindness shown. To give a sense of achievement, cut out the Kindness Club badge and make a Kindness Tree to record every act of kindness your child has shown.

And remember, the more enthusiasm and praise children receive – especially when they've turned a tricky situation around – the more likely they are to make showing kindness a part of every day.

Author Ella Law
Illustrator Laura Vitória Jäger

Designed and packaged by Collaborate

Editor Laura Gilbert
Senior Designer Elle Ward
Consultant Maureen Healy
Production Editor Abi Maxwell
Production Controller John Casey
Jacket Coordinator Magda Pszuk
Deputy Art Director Mabel Chan
Publisher Francesca Young
Publishing Director Sarah Larter

First published in Great Britain in 2023 by
Dorling Kindersley Limited
DK, One Embassy Gardens, 8 Viaduct Gardens,
London, SW11 7BW

The authorised representative in the EEA is
Dorling Kindersley Verlag GmbH. Arnulfstr. 124,
80636 Munich, Germany

Copyright © 2023 Dorling Kindersley Limited
A Penguin Random House Company
10 9 8 7 6 5 4 3 2 1
001–332841–May/2023

All rights reserved.
No part of this publication may be reproduced, stored in or
introduced into a retrieval system, or transmitted, in any form,
or by any means (electronic, mechanical, photocopying,
recording, or otherwise), without the prior written permission
of the copyright owner.

A CIP catalogue record for this book
is available from the British Library.
ISBN: 978-0-2415-8392-0 (Hardback)
ISBN: 978-0-2416-4330-3 (Paperback)

Printed and bound in China

For the curious
www.dk.com

MIX
Paper | Supporting
responsible forestry
FSC™ C018179

FSC
www.fsc.org

This book was made with Forest
Stewardship Council™ certified
paper – one small step in DK's
commitment to a sustainable future.
For more information go to
www.dk.com/our-green-pledge